Published by SYDA Foundation
P.O. Box 600, 371 Brickman Rd., South Fallsburg, NY 12779-0600, USA
(845) 434-2000 *www.siddhayoga.org*

ACKNOWLEDGMENTS
*Heartfelt thanks to all the many people who brought this book to fruition: to the editor, Robyn Jensen; to Manuela
Soares, Sarah Scott, Carolyn Vaughan, and Kathy Morgan, who offered editorial assistance; to Michael Stewart for
design; to the art director, Melanie Hall; to the photographer, Kerry Kehoe; to Carl Turner and Shane Conroy for their
artistic support; to Derek Beecham for technical support; to the production coordinator, Patricia Stratton-Orloske; and
special thanks to Susan Cornelis for the love and talent she offered creating these wonderful illustrations.*
                                                                                  —*Karen Swezey, Managing Editor*

Printed in the United States of America

First published 2002

10 09 08 07 06 05 04 03 02   5 4 3 2 1

ISBN 0-911307-90-7

The Great Hiss

As told by
Gurumayi Chidvilasananda

Illustrated by Susan Cornelis

Foreword

For centuries, animal tales have been used to entertain children around the world. In the West we have Aesop's fables, and in the East there are the famous Panchatantra and other tales. The timeless wisdom of these stories instills in each new generation the moral and spiritual values of community life. As a young girl, Gurumayi grew up hearing these magical stories, and "The Great Hiss" was one of her favorites. As the blessed year 2001 is the Chinese Year of the Snake, it is a fitting time to tell the tale of a snake called Long Fang!

Through her delightful retelling of this classic Indian fable, Gurumayi transports us to Long Fang's world in the Indian countryside. We are moved to laughter and tears at the fate of this arrogant snake who transforms from town bully into a practitioner of nonviolence.

Long Fang's journey begins when he meets a loving monk named Swami Madhavananda, who shows him that being gentle doesn't mean becoming a doormat for others. Rather, gentleness has a strength and integrity all its own, the power to create harmony in the world. Through this children's tale, Gurumayi teaches us all how to navigate the waters of human existence — how to practice nonviolence without forgetting when and how to hiss.

— *Robyn Jensen, Editor*

Once upon a time, there was a big old snake. He lived near a small village called Vajreshwari. The snake's name was Long Fang. He was an ill-tempered fellow with a very low boiling point. He tried to bite anyone who came near him because he had developed a hatred toward people — actually toward anything that moved. If a dry leaf fell, he would strike at it. Even if the wind rustled through the bushes, he would spit venom at it.

Long Fang went out of his way
to torment the farmers and
to scare the village children.

He loved to bully the women who came to draw water from the well. Sneaking up on them, he would lunge forward and attack them. Water would splash everywhere as the women ran for safety clutching their pots. Long Fang had been doing this for years. In fact, he had established a reign of terror in the village.

To appease Long Fang, the villagers had to leave bowls of food and milk outside their doors every day. If they forgot, or left too small a portion, he would lie in wait and take his revenge.

Each day the people spent hours looking for all kinds of colorful, succulent creatures for the menu. The treats had to be his favorites, and woe to the unlucky person who brought him anything boring to eat.

One day, a wandering monk, a swami named Madhavananda, was passing through the village of Vajreshwari on his way to the Devi temple. He was a man who was well-known for his kindness toward all living creatures, and the villagers welcomed him with great reverence.

They felt it was their duty to warn him about Long Fang, so they told him about their troubles with the snake. Much to their relief, Swami Madhavananda offered to look into the matter.

The next morning, he set off down the road.

Suddenly, he heard a loud rustling in the bushes.

There was Long Fang—
coiled and ready to strike—
his muscles tensed, his head
swaying slightly, his tongue
flicking in and out between
two glistening fangs.
For a long time he stared
at Swami Madhavananda.

Then, a most unusual thing
happened.

As Long Fang looked into the eyes of Swami Madhavananda, he saw so much gentleness, so much compassion…

he just couldn't bring himself to bite this tenderhearted being.

Swami Madhavananda calmly walked over to a nearby tree and sat down.
The snake followed him and curled up at his feet. The swami closed his
eyes and began to hum a sweet melody.

It was so soothing to Long Fang's soul. In this way, they spent a pleasant hour sitting quietly together.

Finally, Swami Madhavananda got up to leave. As he put his shawl over his shoulder, he lovingly said, "My friend, stop biting people. It's just not good."

The snake's crusty old heart had become so tender, so gentle in the swami's company, that he could feel the truth of what Madhavananda was saying. The words penetrated his heart, and he agreed to change his ways and stop being mean to people.

A year later, Swami Madhavananda was passing through Vajreshwari once again on his way to the Devi temple. As he walked down the road, he expected to see his old friend Long Fang, but the snake wasn't there.

The swami went looking for him. He went to the tree where they had sat together. He searched on the hillsides and in the fields. He peered into every hole in the ground, calling, "Long Fang! Long Fang, where are you? This is your friend, Madhavananda, who has come back to see you. Please come and say hello!" But there was no sign of Long Fang.

Finally, he came across the snake lying in the rice paddies. He was battered and tattered and covered with wounds. He could hardly breathe. Swami Madhavananda swiftly went down on his knees and asked, "What happened to you, my friend?" Long Fang very slowly opened his eyes and looked up at the holy man. He could barely speak, so he whispered,

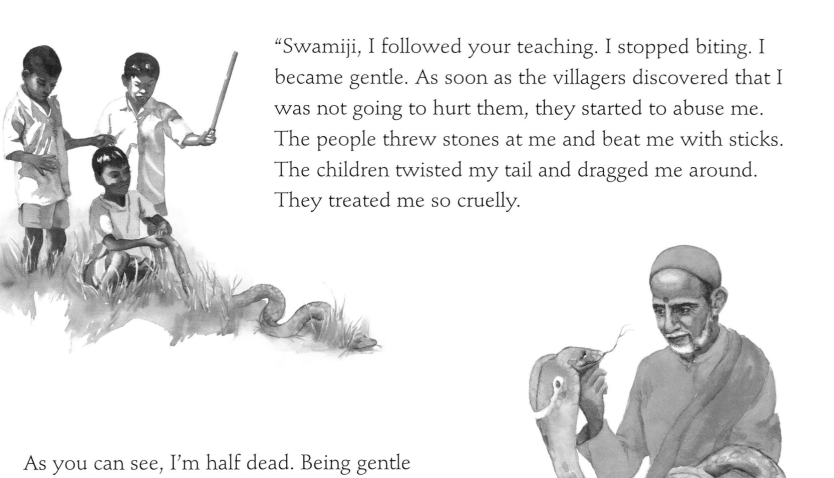

"Swamiji, I followed your teaching. I stopped biting. I became gentle. As soon as the villagers discovered that I was not going to hurt them, they started to abuse me. The people threw stones at me and beat me with sticks. The children twisted my tail and dragged me around. They treated me so cruelly.

As you can see, I'm half dead. Being gentle and not biting anyone hasn't paid off. It has only given others the freedom to take advantage of me."

Swami Madhavananda listened to the snake with all his heart. Then he leaned over and gently patted Long Fang on the back and said, "Brother, I told you not to bite…

He smiled encouragingly at Long Fang. "Come on, show me your hiss." Long Fang slowly raised his head and made a feeble *phsssh…*

"Try it one more time," urged the swami. Little by little, Long Fang drew his poor, bruised body up, and with tremendous effort, he let out a great…

Hiss

"Ha ha! That's it!" cried Madhavananda. "In good time, my friend, your hiss will be heard throughout the entire valley."

So, Long Fang learned to hiss. Whenever he felt he was in danger, he would make a fierce hissing sound. It really worked. People stopped bothering him. And he never hurt anyone, ever again.

In the village of Vajreshwari,
    harmony reigned once again.

Sadgurunath Maharaj Ki Jay

A joyful expression offering love and thanks to God.
In Hindi, one of the languages spoken in India, it means
"Hail to the one who gives the highest knowledge."

About Swami Madhavananda

Swami Madhavananda was born in 1936 in the southern Indian town of Nellore. Swamiji, as he is affectionately called, is one of the monks of Siddha Yoga meditation. He lives in the Siddha Yoga meditation ashram, or spiritual retreat, in Ganeshpuri, India.

Swami Madhavananda had an amazing experience with a cobra when he was young. When he was about a year old, he was playing in the backyard while his mother was doing laundry. At one point, she stepped inside the house for a moment. When she came back, she saw that he was sitting underneath a huge cobra, whose open hood was sheltering his head from the sun. The baby was sitting very still and did not seem scared, so his mother didn't move. After a few minutes, the cobra quietly slithered away into the bushes.

Swamiji continues to have great experiences with cobras. In the Chinese Year of The Snake, 2001, he saw an eight-foot long, golden cobra very near to where this story takes place.

Glossary

Devi Temple:
A holy place in the village of Vajreshwari dedicated to three goddesses. Many pilgrims visit there to express devotion and ask for blessings.

Vajreshwari:
A village in central India, very near the Siddha Yoga meditation ashram in Ganeshpuri. It gets its name from a goddess who has been worshipped there since ancient times.

DATE DUE

GREAT HISS
GURUMAYI CHIDVILASANANDA